WolfWalkers

The Graphic Novel

WolfWalkers

The Graphic Novel

Based on the film by
TOMM MOORE & ROSS STEWART

Adapted by
SAM SATTIN

LB

Little, Brown and Company
New York Boston

About This Book

This book was edited by Rachel Poloski and designed by Ching N. Chan, Maria Caritas, Dwi Febri Novita, Dies Caya, Marsela Giovani of Caravan Studio. The production was supervised by Bernadette Flinn, and the production editor was Lindsay Walter-Greaney. The text was set in Jacoby, and the display type is Wolfwalkers.

© 2020 Wolfwalkers

Illustrations by Tomm Moore and Maria Pareja.

Cover design by Ching N. Chan.

Little, Brown and Company
Hachette Book Group
1290 Avenue of the Americas, New York, NY 10104
Visit us at LBYR.com/Wolfwalkers

First Edition: December 2020

Little, Brown and Company is a division of Hachette Book Group, Inc. The Little, Brown name and logo are trademarks of Hachette Book Group, Inc.

The publisher is not responsible for websites (or their content) that are not owned by the publisher.

Library of Congress Control Number: 2020937579

ISBNs: 978-0-316-46178-8 (hardcover), 978-0-316-42953-5 (paperback), 978-0-316-42949-8 (ebook), 978-0-316-42951-1 (ebook), 978-0-316-42950-4 (ebook)

Printed in China

APS

Hardcover: 10 9 8 7 6 5 4 3 2 1
Paperback: 10 9 8 7 6 5 4 3 2 1

To the amazing wolf pack of artists and production staff who made the movie and this graphic novel possible.

Fadó fadó...

In the Kingdom of Osraighe, there was a tribe
with the power to heal. When Naomh Pádraig
(Saint Patrick) came to tell the people of the new
religion, this tribe stayed apart from the others.
They would not give up the old ways.

When the holy man preached, they howled from
the forest like wolves to remind the people that
there was another, older wisdom in the woods.
Some say Naomh Pádraig cursed them; others that
he blessed them. But the result was the same—for
ever more, they would walk as people by day and
roam as wolves by night.

Leaving their human form behind, any harm or good that befell them as wolves, they felt in their waking form, too. They were a proud breed living with the wild wolves, keeping the peace between man and the wilderness.

But Ireland's neighbors craved her wealth and took most
of her forests for their ships. With the woods gone, the
Wolfwalkers dwindled until only two of their kind remained—
a mother and her daughter. Then a new leader came to
power; he killed the king of England and took the title

Lord Protector.

He swore to tame Ireland more thoroughly than the king
had ever managed, ordering the last of the forest felled and
the wolves destroyed. He brought his army to subjugate
the people and impose with force the order that
had been resisted for so long. Among his
men were a hunter and his daughter,

Robyn Goodfellowe.

CHOP!

GRRRRRr

Huh?

AWWOₒₒ

No...please... I'm sorry....

Vhhhhhmmmm

BA-BONG!

BA-BONG!

They won't stop, love...these new invaders.

You see that, Merlyn? Right on the nose.

Cheep?

Oh, come on! I was aimin' for the nose.

Cheep...

I'm glad you agree.

Robyn?!

Yes, Father.

TUNK

Cheep.

Time to practice our trackin', Merlyn.

Cheep?

Yes! Now stop complainin'.

You track him. I'll follow.

Get yer pickled oysters! Yer whelks and periwinkles! Wash 'em down with a cup of donkey's milk!

Yuk!

Oh, where's he gone?

Excuse me. Pardon me.

Huh?

Robyn...

I was only goin' to track you as far as the gates.

Is that right? You weren't goin' to follow me out and slay a pack of wolves single-handed?

Well, yes! But only because I thought we could hunt them together. Wolves, bears—dragons, even!

Yes, sir.

Stay here, lass.

Wolf! Wolf!

We've got the wolf! We've got the wolf!

Ha! Gotcha now, wolf...

Hey, English girl!

Where do ye think yer goin' dressed like tha'?

Wolf, wolf,
kill the wolf.

Hunt them far
and yonder.

What's goin'
on here?

Soldier!
Leg it!

Why must you
wander off like
that, Robyn?

I was tryin'
to help! And then
there was a boy, and
he said his father
was better than you,
and then he wanted
me crossbow and
then—

Robyn, we are...not so welcome in this land yet.

But I'd be just as safe out here with you.

You're better off to stay home while I'm workin'. It's safe there.

No, Robyn! Stay inside. Do as you're *told.*

SLAM

Look, this evenin', when I'm back...

...you can help me make new arrows.

Then you can tell me your stories of giants and dragons.

Would you like that?

...I suppose so.

Great. Now then, be good.

If he could just see how good I am...

Chirp!

What a good hunter I am...

Then he'd **have** to let me come along.

Cheep?

What are you, Merlyn? A falcon or a chicken?

FSSS

SKREEE!

Merlyn!

AWWOᵒᵒ

Hey! That's my bird. Leave him be!

Stop!

GRAR!

By God, yer one lucky girl, ye know that?

'Twas a Wolfwalker. By Crom...

Now, calm down.

Everyone knows ye can't be cuttin' down their woods! If ye do, they'll get ya. Sure, **that's the deal!**

There's no deal with anyone.

Saint Pádraig made a deal with the old pagans, and now yer breakin' it!

We need to clear the wood.

Did ye not see?

Actually, I did see the wolf attack.

The way them wolves answered her call?!

Them forests is **riddled** with wolves, I tell ye!

Well, it won't be long before the wolves are gone.

It won't be long before they're inside the town walls with the hunger.

No, we'll tame these lands. The Lord Protector has ordered it.

Ah...the great Lord Protector Cromwell... Renowned fer bein' so true to his word!

Hilarious.

At least the old king kept us safe. This one? He's just an upstart. **Lord Protector?!**

snort

If you have grievances, you should speak with me directly.

Wha?! Now, I, eh...

I did nathin' wrong!

Another wolf attack?

Aye, my lord.

This is a joke! By Crom! The devil take yer head! May Pádraig drive ye back to England, ye snakes!

A few more like him and we'll have another rebellion on our hands.

If we don't clear the trees, the farmers cannot work the land.

And the woodcutters cannot clear the trees with these wolves.

Onward!

Hey. **Psst.** Girl.

The one who took yer bird. I seen her before—

A while back...with her ma. Cross me heart—she's one o' them **Wolfwalkers.**

Y'know, the ones that can talk to wolves like.

Sure, it's mad stuff, but it's true!

Wolfwalkers?

FRSSSH

Merlyn...

Merrrrrllyn!

FRSSSH

FRSSSH

CHEEEEEEP!

Merlyn!

Look at you! You're...You're good as new, aren't you?!

I'm so glad you're not hurt. And your wing's all healed. How did *that* happen?

It was the girl, wasn't it?

Cheep!

What did she do?

I was afraid she was gonna eat you!

Chirp?

Oh, it doesn't matter. You're safe now.

Cheep?
Chirp!

Cheep
chirp!

Cheep!

Huh?

Merlyn, stop that!

Stay back now. Back!

I'll shoot.

What the—?

WHOOOOSH

Oh...no...

VHMMM

Wha...?

Now give us a look at ye.

Are ye seein' things?

Aggh! Get **off** me!

Stop it! Yech!

Smells like townie...Any extra fur?

Hey, that's mine!

Get off me!

Will ye stop?! Lemme fix it!

SNAP!

AAAAGHHH!!

Caught again? Some hunter...

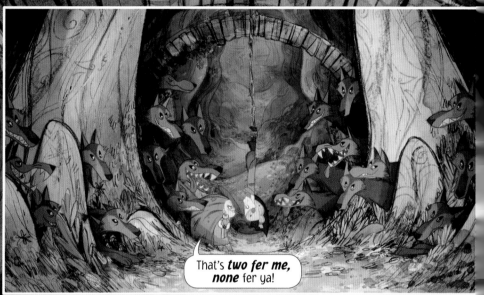

That's **two fer me, none** fer ya!

Stop bein' so **annoyin'.** It's not funny, you know.

UGGGH. LET. ME. DOWN!

Alright, townie, if ye say so!

Huh...

That was too close.

What are ya so scared of? We have a **pack o' wolves** with us!

WHAM

Hey! I told ye! **Ye can't go out in the daytime.** Ma said so.

Go back to bed!

RARRRRRR

BAAAAAA!

BAAAAAA!

I have to tell my father about you.

He didn't know...

SNAP!

We didn't know that Wolfwalkers were real... That you were people.

CRCK
CRCK

Father?
Father?

We need to tidy
this place up before
he gets back.

"My, Robyn.
This place is
sparklin'."

Thank you, Father, take a seat. Put up your feet.

"Don't mind if I do, lass."

Hard day huntin'?

"Aye, not a sniff of wolf out there."

Well...what if I told you I can get all the wolves to leave and we don't even have to kill them?

"I'd say you're tellin' tall tales again."

Oooh, but I'm not.

Now, promise me you won't get angry....

"I promise."

You see, I met a girl in the forest who has magic healin' powers. She healed Merlyn. And she's a **Wolfwalker.**

"A Wolfwalker?!"

It's true. When she sleeps, she turns into a wolf.

She can talk to the wolves. Smell and act like them, too. Her and her mother were goin' to take the wolves away, but her mother went missin'.

"Missin'? Poor thing."

I know, but if we can help her find her mother—

then they can all leave the forest together and you will have done your duty to the Lord Protector.

"Oh, brilliant, lass. Absolutely brilliant. Thank you. Our problems are solved."

We can go back to how things used to be—

CLICK

CREEEAK

Ah, my girl. Come here to me.

Oh! Nice to have a new girl joinin' us.

Keep an eye on her. She's to work the full day.

Remember, Robyn. Work is prayer.

'Tis alright, child. I was only half yer age when I started here. Just do as yer told now and ye'll be grand.

Ah now, there ye are.

Did ye see yer new friend again?

No, I can't get out...I have to work in the castle...

I think...I think I heard—

Robyn!

Come in!

You will catch your death out there!

Well, now. Are ye a hunter or a housemaid?

SLAM

Work is prayer, Robyn.

Then I prayed the whole Bible.

Good lass.

This is still new for you.

It is a righteous life for a young lady.

Well, it's no life for me!

I can get the Wolfwalkers to leave.

You just need to listen t' me—

Robyn Goodfellowe, enough of your stories.

I can go look for her—

You must do as you're told! No more fairy tales!

But—

No "buts'"!

WOLFWALKERS ARE NOT REAL!

Now go to bed.

Hey! Calm down and give her room.

Go back to bed!

Now I see ye like this, it's flippin' great.

I thought we were the last ones.

It's *great?!* I'm a *Wolfwalker!*

I know! Ma said this would be bad.

Like, never to bite anyone...but...I *love* it! It's smashin'!

This is bad. I'll get killed like this. What about my body?

It's asleep, nice and cozy. Look...

...yer a wolf when ye sleep. A girl when yer awake.

No big deal!

But the soldiers.

And—and my father...

Don't worry about that.

Learn how to be a wolf first! Come on!

Why do ye **want** to be a human?

Bein' a wolf is **way** better. I'll show ye.

Can ye smell me?

Of course! Everybody can!

TWOO!

Wolf!

That scent...
I knew it!

Made a new friend, Ma. She's a townie...but a nice one.

Her name is Robyn...

She's taller than me, but *I'm* stronger. And she brushed me hair and gave me this flower.

And she's from a place called England. And we're gonna meet by the oak tree tomorrow.

And she promised to help. And... and...

SNIFFLE...

Where are ye? Ye promised ye'd come back. But it's been so long now. Are ye lost?

Has somethin' happened to ye?

Robyn will help me find ye, Ma. She promised. There's two of us now....

Mebh...

CAW!

Robyn? Time for work!

Robyn, whats keeping ya?

Birdy! About time!

Where's Robyn?

Chirp.

What d'ye mean she can't come outta the town?

I'm not leavin'! She promised. Help me find her, Merlyn.

Chirp.

Where were ya?

Mebh! What are you doin' here?

I waited fer *ages.*

You're supposed to be gone. I sent Merlyn to tell you.

What's that, girl? Who are ye talkin' to?

Oh, nobody...

You must go, Mebh! Lead the pack away to safety.

I told ya! I'm **not leavin'** without me ma!

Ye promised!

Mebh, you have to listen to me. You must leave the forest, take the wolves, and go!

Good, that's enough. Step away. Return to your positions.

What's in the cage?

Look at that, the whole town is here.

Look, they're bringin' a big cage out! What's in the cage?

A big stage, eh? What's he at?

Somethin' to do with the wolf everyone's talkin' about.

Listen, he's talkin' now! What's his plan—he's been promisin' everythin', but we got nothin' so far.

Yeah, a wolf runnin' through the streets—nearly ate me Jimmy.

Me ma's here! Get off of me!

Mebh, **STOP!** Please...

Please! I need me ma!

This is for your own good.

♪♪ Wolf, wolf, kill the wolf... ♪

Now. Reveal the beast!

Are ye mad, man?

GASP!

Don't open that door, ye loon!

Watch out! She's wild!

Hey, watch it!

Where's she goin'?!

I am a Wolfwalker! I'm gettin' me wolves. I'm comin' back fer me ma. Then...

Ouch!

...WE'LL ATE YE ALL!

AWWOoo

Huh? A Wolfwalker?

She's callin' the pack!

AWWOoo.

Bloody hell! Listen to that! It's true! They are comin'!

AWWOoo.

We are done for!

Do not fear wild girls and wolves.

Because *tonight* we put an end to this. *I* will burn this forest to the ground.

I will lead cannons to the den of these beasts and send them all to hell.

No!

Get home!

Lock your doors!

Can't control them wolves.

Prepare a squadron.

We shall prevail. It is the Lord's will!

Goodfellowe. What have you become? You can't even catch a little girl?

Sir, I—

Prove yourself a worthy soldier tonight or tomorrow you are in **chains.**

Now, put an end to that wild beast!

What cannot be **tamed** must be **destroyed!**

AGGHH! The wolf, it's out!

Watch out— the beast!

Ma.

Mebh, love...

Ma, yer back!

I thought I would never see ye again.

Until this one freed me.

Robyn, no. Stay.

No, Father! Let me go! **I have to help her...** She's dyin'. I have to go with them.

No, Robyn, **why?!** I don't understand!

Don't you see? I'm one of them.

I'm a Wolfwalker.

No, Robyn. Please...

I can't let you go.

Father...

VHMMMM

Robyn!
ROBYN!

SNAP!

A fresh track. Move on!

Burn it all!

VHMMMMM

Ma!

I can't, Ma, **I can't.**
I'm not strong enough.

Please...
tell me what
to do.

The pack!

I need
the pack!

AWWOₒₒₒ

That wild girl is calling them!

We ain't got a chance.

It's a Wolfwalker!

AWWOₒₒₒ

It ain't natural!

What do you think you're doing?! Get back to your positions!

That's not normal wolves, sir, we're gone!

RUN!

Cowards!

Robyn...!

Where's Robyn?!

AWWOoo

Robyn?
Robyn!

Robyn, get up. Run!

Enough, Goodfellowe.

CHEEEEEP!

Skree!

Aggh! Foul bird!

CLANK

CRUNCH

Goodfellowe!

PTANG!

Father, you're one of us now.

AWWOoo..

We have to help Mebh.

Please, Ma, don't go. Don't go. Don't leave me again....

Mebh...

Robyn...I tried...I really tried, but...

I'm just not strong enough. I need her....

I can help.

Like I promised...
There's two of us now.

Yeh...There's
two of us.

Follow me...

VHHHHMMMM

AWWOₒₒ

AWWOₒₒ

Dylan Vaughan

Tomm Moore is the cofounder and Creative Director of Cartoon Saloon. Tomm directed *The Secret of the Kells* and *Song of the Sea*, both nominated for the Academy Award for Best Animated Feature.

Ross Stewart has been painting, illustrating, designing, and working in animation for over twenty years. Ross has worked on three Oscar nominated movies: *The Secret of the Kells* (Art Director), *Song of the Sea* (concept artist), and *ParaNorman* (visual development). He has also illustrated books and literature for a variety of publishers. He is a nature lover and would gladly sit under an oak tree all day long.

Tomm and Ross codirected *WolfWalkers*, their latest feature film.

Anna Stark

Samuel Sattin is a writer and coffee addict. He is the words behind the Glint trilogy, *Bezkamp*, *Legend*, and *The Silent End*. His work has appeared or been featured in *The Nib*, *The Atlantic*, NPR, and elsewhere. He holds an MFA in Comics from California College of the Arts and has a creative writing MFA from Mills College. Residing in Oakland, California, he sometimes teaches at the California College of the Arts and lives with his wife/assassin and two cats.

Acknowledgments

As a fan of graphic novels from an early age, the visual language of the medium has been a part of my work as a director since the beginning. For *WolfWalkers*, Ross and I drew inspiration from many of our favorite creators and even incorporated graphic novel-style compositions and scene layouts into the film itself, so it was especially exciting for me to be part of adapting our film to the page. We even added some original pages detailing the movie's backstory and the legend of the Wolfwalkers as a bonus to the readers.

I would like to dedicate this graphic novel to the amazing crew who worked with us on the animated feature *WolfWalkers* since so much of their artwork is the basis of everything you will see in the book. I would also like to thank Megan, Rachel, and everyone at Little, Brown Books for Young Readers for their patience and enthusiasm for this adaptation, especially Ching, who made such beautiful layouts and did such a wonderful job designing the book.

Not forgetting, of course, special thanks are due to Sam Sattin, who has done such an excellent job of adapting the script and film for this graphic novel and our team in the Saloon: Desirée, Brian, and especially Maria, who was the not only super fast on the adaptation pages and the original artwork we created for this book but is also one of the most talented artists with whom I've had the pleasure of collaborating.

—Tomm Moore

Cartoon Saloon

WolfWalkers

www.cartoonsaloon.ie

Concept artwork by Alice Dieudonne